This Little Tiger book
belongs to:

*For Lentil, and all the adventures*
*that await you*
*- S C*

*For all my girlfriends who have kindness*
*in their heart and DIY in their soul!*
*- C P*

LITTLE TIGER PRESS LTD,
an imprint of the Little Tiger Group
1 Coda Studios,
189 Munster Road, London SW6 6AW
www.littletiger.co.uk
First published in Great Britain 2019
This edition published 2020

Text by Suzanne Chiew
Text copyright © Little Tiger Press Ltd 2019
Illustrations copyright © Caroline Pedler 2019

Caroline Pedler has asserted her rights to be
identified as the illustrator of this work under
the Copyright, Designs and Patents Act, 1988

A CIP catalogue record for this book is available from the British Library

Printed in China • LTP/1800/3052/1119

2 4 6 8 10 9 7 5 3 1

# Badger AND THE Great ADVENTURE

Suzanne Chiew • Caroline Pedler

LITTLE TIGER

LONDON

One crisp autumn afternoon, Badger sat
in his cosy home, knitting a brand new scarf.
But a great commotion outside made him stop.
    "What's all the rumpus?" he wondered, rushing
to the door.

In the sunshine stood Hedgehog and Rabbit with
three little birds chirping noisily on the ground.
"Badger! What should we do?" cried Hedgehog.
"These poor birds have been separated from their flock!"
"They were flying south for winter," explained Rabbit,
"when the youngest hurt her wing."

Badger picked up the littlest bird. "Oh dear! That wing needs time to heal," he said. "Why don't you stay with me until you're strong enough to fly?"

"Thank you! Thank you! That's most kind!" tweeted the birds.

Winter arrived, bringing with it
blankets of snow, but the three little
birds stayed safe and warm inside
Badger's house.

Every morning the birds sang
Badger a merry tune.

Each day was
filled with laughter
and cheer.

And every evening
they shared stories
by the fire.

One morning, Badger woke to find
the birds singing louder than ever.

"Spring is here!" they chirped.

"And look! I can fly again!" peeped
the littlest bird.

But after a short while in
the air she fluttered to
the ground.

That evening, Badger found her perched sadly by the window.

"Our flock will soon be passing on their way back home," she sniffed. "How will we join them if I can't fly very far?"

"Don't worry," smiled Badger. "Every problem has a solution!" And his eyes twinkled with a new idea.

The next day, Hedgehog and Rabbit came over
to hear all about Badger's plan.

"Ooh! What's that?" asked Rabbit, as Badger
laid out his sketches.

"A flying machine," explained Badger. "Swift and
speedy, to help us reach the flock!"

"Hooray!" cheered Rabbit and Hedgehog,
and they all set to work.

They measured . . .

and sawed . . .

and glued long into
the evening.
    "Many hands make
light work," sang Badger.
"It's nearly finished!"

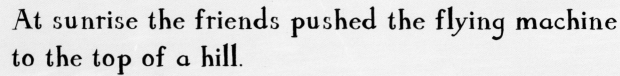

At sunrise the friends pushed the flying machine
to the top of a hill.

"Quick, jump in!" yelled Badger as it started
rolling down the grassy slope. "Here we go!"

And with one last BUMP . . .

. . . the machine took to the skies.

"Wow!" gasped Hedgehog. "Flying
is incredible!"

"You can see the whole woodland,"
beamed Rabbit. "Look – there's Mole's
house, and that's where Mouse lives!"

On they soared, over rivers and rolling hills.
Suddenly, the littlest bird began to chirp.
   "Our flock!" she cried, spotting
her friends in the distance.
   "Time to catch them up!" declared
Badger, and they raced ahead.

"Where have you been?" cried the flock,
fluttering with joy. "We've been so worried!"

"My wing was hurt, but I'm better now,"
laughed the littlest bird. "And it's all
thanks to our new friends."

Soon it was time for
the flock to continue its
journey home.
"Safe travels!" waved Badger.
"We'll miss you!" twittered the
little birds. "Goodbye! Goodbye!"

"What a special day,"
cheered Hedgehog as
they flew back towards
the woodland.

But suddenly a crash of thunder made
the flying machine rattle and shake.
"Hold tight!" warned Badger.
"I can't look!" gulped Rabbit.
Lightning lit up the sky as they
steered through the stormy clouds.
"Get ready for a bumpy landing,"
Badger hollered, and down they swooped.

At last the friends were back on safe ground.
"What an adventure!" said Rabbit. "But I'm
glad we're home."

Later, cosy and dry in his house,
Badger thought of the happy times
he had shared with the little birds.
"I shall miss them," he sighed.

As the days passed, spring turned into summer and bees buzzed happily in the woodland. Badger kept busy in his garden, but every now and then he would think of the little birds and smile.

Autumn returned,
bringing with it colourful
leaves, golden afternoons,
and a big surprise . . .

"You're back!" cried Badger, hearing a familiar chirpy tune.

"Of course!" tweeted the birds. "We have so much to tell you!"

And from that year on, when the autumn leaves began to fall, Badger enjoyed a visit from his very special friends.

# More great adventures with Little Tiger!

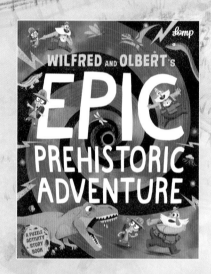

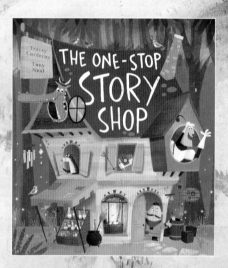

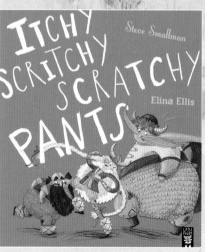

For information regarding any of the above titles or for our catalogue, please contact us:
Little Tiger Press Ltd, 1 Coda Studios, 189 Munster Road, London SW6 6AW
Tel: 020 7385 6333 • E-mail: contact@littletiger.co.uk • www.littletiger.co.uk